Grumpy Bunny's™ SNOWY DAY

by Justine Korman

illustrated by Lucinda McQueen

D1408665

Troll

For Monkey Boy,
who makes every day fun!
—J.K.

For Kaylee and Jamie,
who always enjoy their snowy days
Love, Lucy

Text copyright © 1997 by Justine Korman.
Illustrations copyright © 1997 by Lucinda McQueen.

Published by WhistleStop, an imprint and registered trademark
of Troll Communications L.L.C.

Grumpy Bunny is a trademark of Justine Korman, Lucinda McQueen,
and Troll Communications L.L.C.

Printed in the United States of America.
ISBN 0-8167-4379-7

10   9   8   7   6   5   4   3   2   1

One morning, Hopper woke up to a winter wonderland. But was the grumpy bunny happy? Of course not!

"Boots and bother," Hopper grumbled. He hated all the fuss of snow. And most of all, Hopper hated shoveling!

While he ate breakfast, Hopper listened to the radio:
"Due to last night's storm, the following schools will be closed: Bitty Bunny Preschool, Easter Bunny Elementary School . . ."

The grumpy bunny sighed with relief. At least he wouldn't have to go to school and be pestered by a bunch of excited kinderbunnies.

Hopper pulled on his coat, boots, hat, scarf, and mittens. "What a lot of stuff to wear," he complained. "Once I get all this shoveling done, I'll come inside and have a nice, quiet day at home."

But as soon as the grumpy bunny stepped outside, he was surrounded by snow-happy kinderbunnies.

Little Muffin laughed. "Isn't it beautiful?"

"Happy snow day, Hopper," Peter called.

Hopper grunted. He saw nothing happy about having to shovel.

Suddenly, his ears flew up with an idea. What if he got the kinderbunnies to shovel for him? After all, those silly little bunnies found fun in everything. They would probably even enjoy shoveling.

Hopper turned to his students.

"Hot chocolate all around—if you shovel my walk," he proposed.

The kinderbunnies looked skeptical. "We can get hot chocolate at home without shoveling," Muffin pointed out.

Peter thought for a moment, then he smiled at Hopper. "We'll shovel your walk, *if* you take us sledding down the Big Hill first."

"I don't know," muttered Hopper. "That doesn't sound like such a good idea to me."

"Please!" said all the kinderbunnies together. "Pretty please with marshmallows on top!"

"Oh, all right," Hopper grumped. "Let's get this over with." He and the kinderbunnies tramped through the sparkling snow to the Big Hill.

"Okay, hurry up and have fun!"
Hopper announced when they reached the top of the Big Hill.
"We won't be here long!"

But no one was listening. The kinderbunnies were already
sledding down the long, steep hill, squealing with glee.

Hopper watched their first few runs. None of the bunnies was going as far or as fast as he knew he could.

He reached for Peter's sled. "Here, let me show you the right way to do it," he said.

Hopper ran as fast as he could, then flopped onto the sled. Soon he was whooshing full-speed down the Big Hill.

By the time Hopper saw the snowdrift, it was too late. He wiped out in a cascade of powdery snow. It was wonderful!

Hopper couldn't wait to go again.
As he pulled the sled back up the hill,
his ears bounced merrily with
each step.

Finally, everyone was all tuckered out. "Let's go shovel
the walk now," said Hopper, and all the kinderbunnies agreed.
But on the shortcut back to Hopper's house, the group
passed a frozen pond.

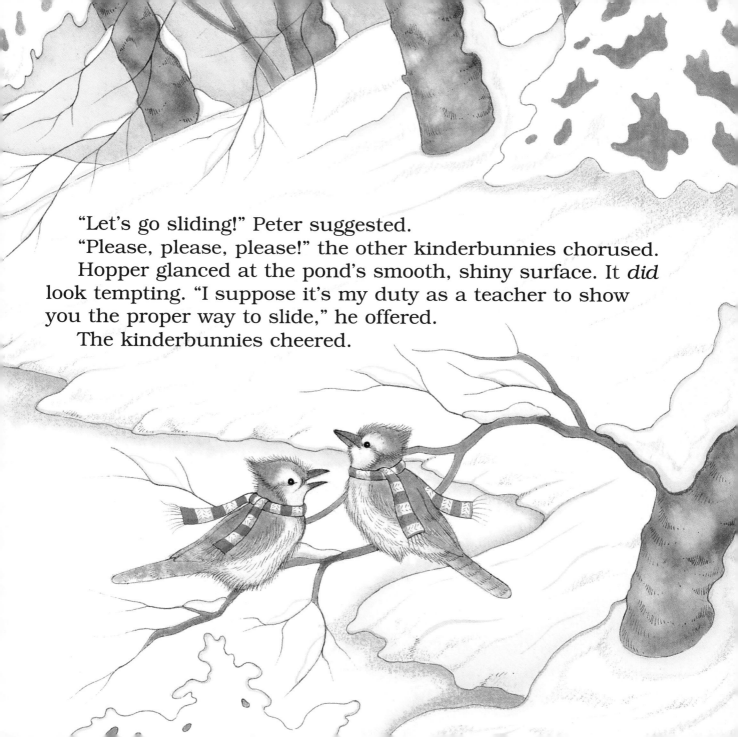

"Let's go sliding!" Peter suggested.

"Please, please, please!" the other kinderbunnies chorused.

Hopper glanced at the pond's smooth, shiny surface. It *did* look tempting. "I suppose it's my duty as a teacher to show you the proper way to slide," he offered.

The kinderbunnies cheered.

Hopper got a running start. When he had picked up enough speed, he jumped onto the ice and slid. The world rushed past him in a blur of shimmering snow. For a moment, he felt as if he were flying!

Then his foot hit a rock poking up through the ice. Hopper
stuck out his arms, wiggled his ears, and recovered his
balance. "I've still got it!" he cried triumphantly as he—

FA-WHUMP! Hopper felt hard, cold ice under his tail.

As he skidded to a stop, he heard a funny sound: *FA-FA-FA . . .WHUMP, WHUMP, WHUMP!*

The kinderbunnies who had been sliding behind Hopper tumbled into one another like falling dominoes.

Flopsy laughed, and everyone joined in—even Hopper!

The group left the pond and began to walk back to
Hopper's house. But all that deep white snow was just
too enticing.

"Let's have a snowball fight!" Muffin shouted.

The other bunnies ran to a big drift to build their forts.

Hopper forgot all about shoveling. He loved snowball fights!

The grumpy bunny cleared his throat. "I suppose I *should*
teach you the right way to build a snow fort."

He showed the kinderbunnies how to shape mounds of
snow into sturdy shelters.

After Hopper and the kinderbunnies had built their forts, he taught them how to pack a perfect snowball.

Soon the bunnies were caught up in a fierce battle. Snowballs whizzed through the air. Bunnies from one fort tried to sneak up on the other. Walls were battered and rebuilt. Targets were bombarded. Mittens were soaked.

Two kinderbunnies grabbed big round
snowballs and came running at Hopper.
"Watch this dodge," he said, diving to one side.
Suddenly, he found himself staring up at the sky.
Hopper had fallen backward onto the soft snow.

He waved his arms up and down and scissored
his legs in and out.

"Snow angels!" the kinderbunnies exclaimed. They all
fell down in the snow and joined in.

Hopper and the kinderbunnies made snow angels all
the way back to Hopper's house.

"Now it really is time for shoveling," Hopper declared.
With all the kinderbunnies pitching in, shoveling wasn't
boring at all. In fact, Hopper had to admit—it was fun!

First, they had a speed-shoveling race. Then there was a contest to see who could throw snow the highest and who could pitch it the farthest.

Once all the snow was in a giant heap,
Hopper looked at it and had a wonderful
thought. "Let's build a snowbunny!"
The kinderbunnies were happy
to help.

In no time at all, the spectacular statue was done. But something was missing. "I think he needs some friends," Hopper suggested.

The bunnies worked quickly, and soon the big snowbunny was surrounded by lots of little snowbunnies. Hopper grinned. "That's much better."

"I sure hope it snows tomorrow!" Daisy said.

"Me, too!" Flopsy cried.

"Me, three!" the other bunnies cheered.

And to his amazement, Hopper agreed. "I have an idea," he said. "Let's do a snowdance."

Peter was confused. "A snowdance?"

"You know—like a raindance, only for snow," Flopsy explained.

But Hopper had already begun. He weaved between the snow-covered trees, throwing his head back to look at the sky.

They danced till they were dizzy and all the parents throughout the woods started calling the kinderbunnies to come home.

"Thanks for a wonderful day!" the kinderbunnies said as they hopped away.

"Thank *you!*" said Hopper.

And as he watched them leave, Hopper remembered a rhyme he'd learned back when *he* was a kinderbunny at Easter Bunny Elementary School:

> *No matter what the weather brings,*
> *an Easter Bunny makes it spring.*
> *Find sunshine in every day—*
> *That's the Easter Bunny way!*